How Chipmunk Got His Stripes

A TALE OF BRAGGING AND TEASING

As told by
Joseph Bruchac & James Bruchac
Pictures by Jose Aruego & Ariane Dewey

PUFFIN BOOKS

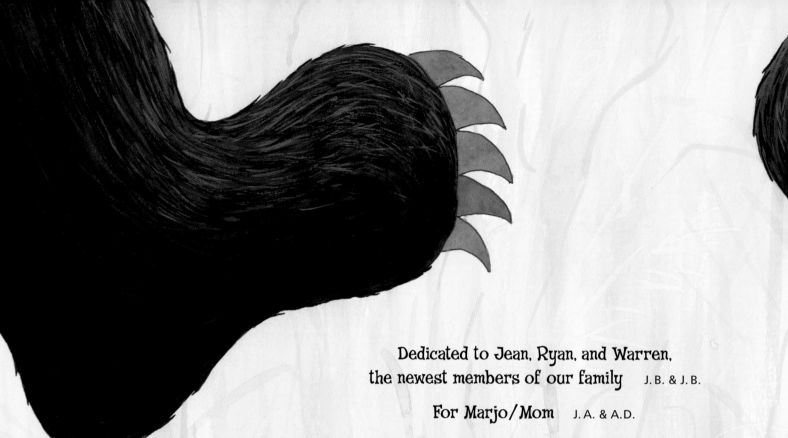

Dedicated to Jean, Ryan, and Warren,
the newest members of our family J.B. & J.B.

For Marjo/Mom J.A. & A.D.

PUFFIN BOOKS
Published by the Penguin Group
Penguin Putnam Books for Young Readers,
345 Hudson Street, New York, New York 10014, U.S.A.
Penguin Books Ltd, 80 Strand, London WC2R ORL, England
Penguin Books Australia Ltd, Ringwood, Victoria, Australia
Penguin Books Canada Ltd, 10 Alcorn Avenue, Toronto, Ontario, Canada M4V 3B2
Penguin Books (N.Z.) Ltd, 182-190 Wairau Road, Auckland 10, New Zealand

Penguin Books Ltd, Registered Offices: Harmondsworth, Middlesex, England

First published in the United States of America by Dial Books for Young Readers,
a division of Penguin Putnam Inc., 2001
Published by Puffin Books, a division of Penguin Putnam Books for Young Readers, 2003

10 9 8 7 6 5

Text copyright © Joseph Bruchac and James Bruchac, 2001
Pictures copyright © Jose Aruego and Ariane Dewey, 2001
All rights reserved

THE LIBRARY OF CONGRESS HAS CATALOGED THE DIAL EDITION AS FOLLOWS:
Bruchac, Joseph, date.
How Chipmunk got his stripes: a tale of bragging and teasing/
retold by Joseph Bruchac and James Bruchac;
pictures by Jose Aruego and Ariane Dewey.—1st ed.
p. cm.
Summary: When Bear and Brown Squirrel have a disagreement about whether Bear can stop
the sun from rising, Brown Squirrel ends up with claw marks on his back and becomes
Chipmunk, the striped one.
ISBN: 0-8037-2404-7 (hc)
1. Indians of North America—Folklore. 2. Tales—East (U.S.)
[1. Indians of North America—Folklore. 2. Chipmunks—Folklore. 3. Folklore—North America.]
I. Bruchac, James. II. Aruego, Jose, ill. III. Dewey, Ariane, ill. IV. Title.
E98.F6 B89343 2001   398.24'529364'08997—dc21   99-016793

Puffin Books ISBN 0-14-250021-6

Printed in The United States of America

Authors' Notes

The story of how Chipmunk got his stripes is still widely told by Native American storytellers along the East Coast. I've been telling this story myself for over twenty-five years. It is hard for me to recall when I first heard it told. Over fifteen years ago I heard it told as a Cherokee tale by Robert White Eagle, a powwow emcee, at the Otsiningo Pow Wow in Binghamton. I heard another version of the story twenty years ago from my dear friend and teacher, the late Maurice Dennis of the Abenaki nation.

Such modern Mohawk tradition bearers as Ray Fadden and Tom Porter know their own versions of this tale. In fact, the earliest written version of the story that I've located is of Iroquois origin. It can be found in Arthur Parker's wonderful collection *Seneca Myths and Folk Tales*, published in 1923.

As is the case with many of the old stories, I feel that I've learned more about it over the years. It has evolved gradually into its present form, which is longer and more detailed than the very brief telling collected by Parker. It is even very different from a briefer telling of my own that I included in my collection *Iroquois Stories: Heroes and Heroines, Monsters and Magic* (The Crossing Press, 1985).

—*Joseph Bruchac*

As a child, I heard this story from my father many times, but it took on new life for me after I began my own storytelling career and saw how young audiences reacted to it. In particular, the dialogue between the bear and the brown squirrel developed as I told the story hundreds of times to children.

—*James Bruchac*

One autumn day long ago, Bear was out walking. As he walked, he began to brag:

"I am Bear. I am the biggest
of all the animals. Yes, I am!
I am Bear. I am the strongest
of all the animals. Yes, I am!
I am Bear. I am the loudest
of all the animals. Yes, I am!
I am Bear, I am Bear.
I can do anything. Yes, I can!"

As soon as Bear said those words, a little voice spoke up from the ground.

"Can you really do anything?"

Bear looked down. He saw a little brown squirrel, standing on his hind legs.

"Can you really do anything?" Brown Squirrel asked again.

Bear stood up very tall. "I am Bear. I can do anything. Yes, I can!"

"Can you tell the sun not to rise tomorrow morning?" Brown Squirrel asked.

"I have never tried that before. But I am Bear. I can do that. Yes, I can!"

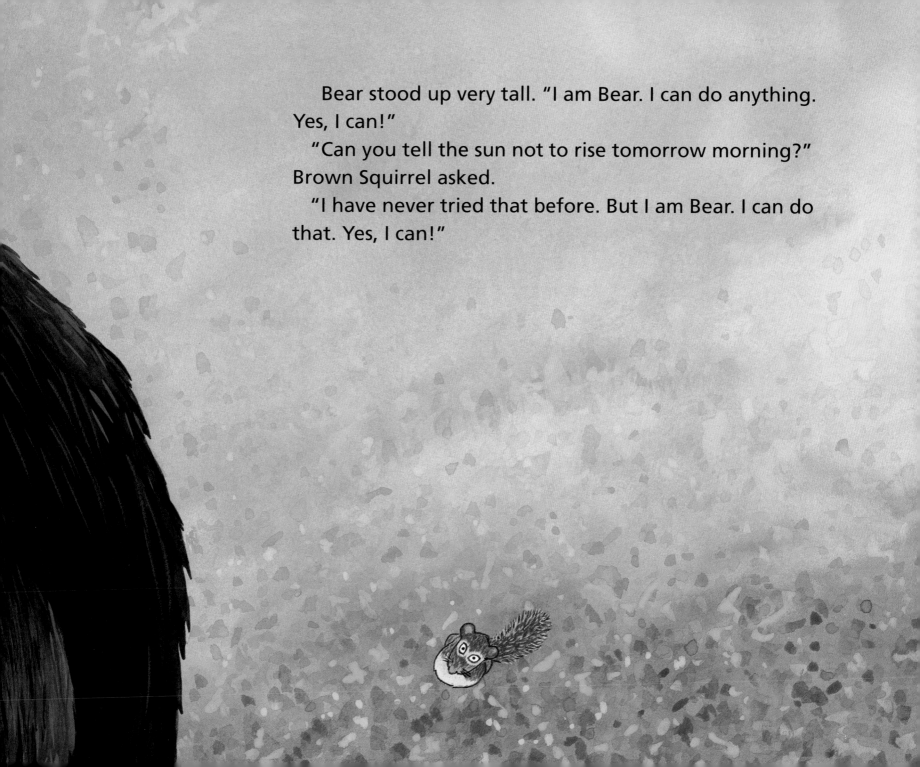

Bear turned west to face the sun. It was the time when the sun always goes down. Bear stood up to his full height and spoke in a loud voice.

"SUN, DO NOT COME UP TOMORROW."

At his words, the sun began to disappear behind the hills.

"You see?" Bear said. "Sun is afraid of me. He is running away."

"But will the sun come up tomorrow?" Brown Squirrel asked.

"No," Bear answered. "The sun will not come up!"

Then Bear turned to face east, the direction where the sun always used to come up. He sat down. Little Brown Squirrel sat down beside him. All that night, they did not sleep. All that night, Bear kept saying these words:

"The sun will not come up, hummph!
The sun will not come up, hummph!"

But as the night went on, little Brown Squirrel began to say something, too. He said these words:

"The sun is going to rise, oooh!
The sun is going to rise, oooh!"

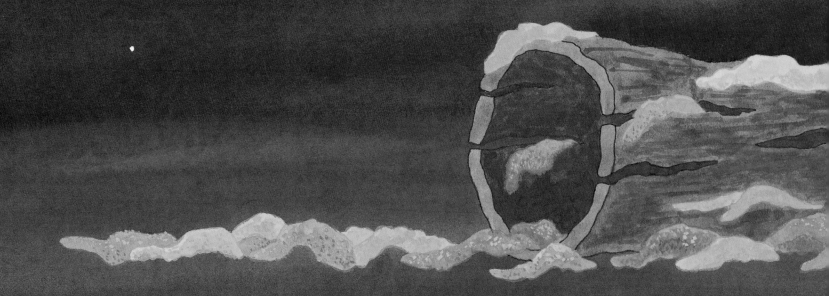

All through the night, they sat there. One by one, other animals gathered around them. Fox and Wolf, Deer and Moose, Rabbit and Porcupine, Hawk and Owl, Otter and Beaver, Frog and Turtle, and even the little mice came. They wanted to see who would be right, Bear or Brown Squirrel.
This is what the other animals heard:

"The sun will not come up, hummph!"
"The sun is going to rise, oooh!"
"The sun will not come up, hummph!"
"The sun is going to rise, oooh!"

Finally, it was just before dawn, the time when the sun always used to come up.

"Look," said Turtle, "a little bit of red is starting to show."

"Yes," said Owl. "I believe the sun will rise today."

Bear only chanted louder:

"The sun will not come up, hummph!"

But right next to him, little Brown Squirrel piped up:

"The sun is going to rise, oooh!"

And the sun came up. The birds sang their welcoming songs. The bright light of the new day spread over the land. Everyone was happy except for one animal. That animal was Bear. He sat there with his head down and a grumpy look on his face.

The happiest animal of all was little Brown Squirrel. "The sun came up," he chirped. "The sun came up, the sun came up, the sun came up."

Brown Squirrel was so happy, he forgot what his wise old grandmother had told him when he was very young.

"Brown Squirrel," his grandmother had said, "it is good to be right about something. But when someone else is wrong, it is not a good idea to tease him."

Now little Brown Squirrel began to tease Bear.

"Bear is foolish, the sun came up.
Bear is silly, the sun came up.
Bear is stupid, the sun—"

WHOMP!

Bear's big paw came down on little Brown Squirrel, pinning him to the ground. Bear leaned over and opened his huge mouth.

"Yes," Bear growled. "The sun did come up. Yes, I do look foolish. But you will not live to see another sunrise. You will not ever tease anyone else again, because I, Bear, am going to eat you."

Brown Squirrel thought fast. "You are right to eat me," he said. "I was wrong to tease you. I would like to say I am sorry before you eat me. But you are pressing down on me so hard that I cannot say anything. I cannot say anything at all. I cannot even breathe. If you would lift up your paw just a little bit, then I could take a deep breath and apologize before you eat me."

"That is a good idea," Bear said. "I would like to hear you apologize before I eat you."

So Bear lifted up his paw. But instead of apologizing, Brown Squirrel ran. He ran as fast as he could toward the pile of stones where he had his home. He had a tunnel under those stones and a nice warm burrow deep underground.

Little Brown Squirrel's grandmother stood there in the door waiting for him.

"Hurry, Brown Squirrel," she called. "Hurry, hurry!"

Little Brown Squirrel dove for the door to his home. But Bear was faster than he looked. He grabbed for little Brown Squirrel with his big paw. Bear's long, sharp claws scratched Brown Squirrel's back from the top of his head to the tip of his tail.

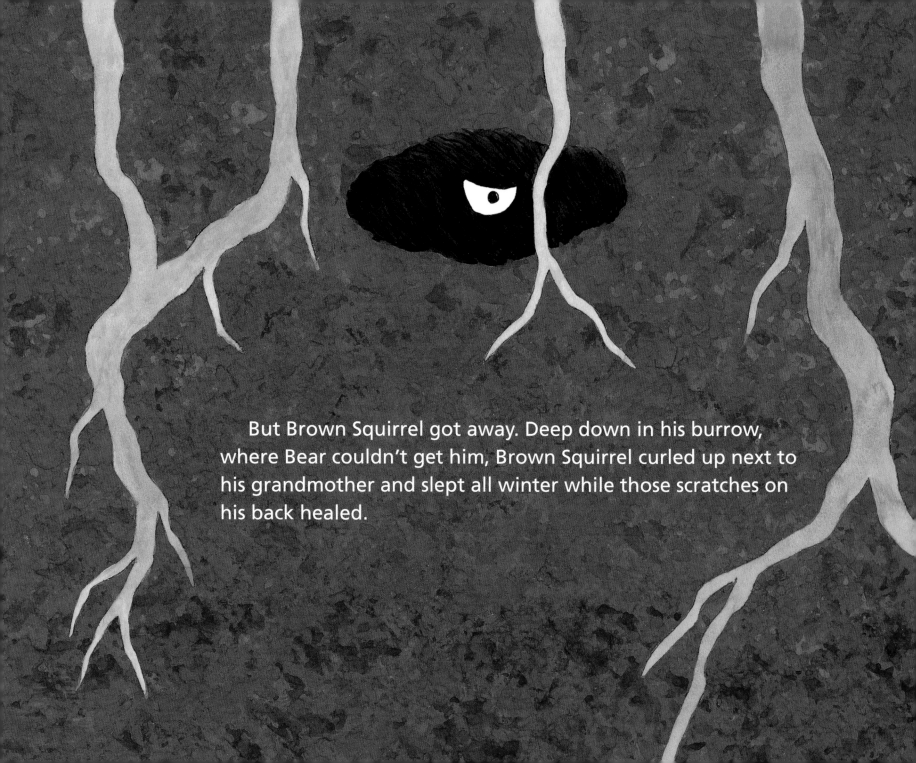

But Brown Squirrel got away. Deep down in his burrow, where Bear couldn't get him, Brown Squirrel curled up next to his grandmother and slept all winter while those scratches on his back healed.

When spring came again, little Brown Squirrel came out of his hole and looked at himself. There were long pale stripes all the way down his back where Bear had scratched him. He was Brown Squirrel no longer. He was now Chipmunk, the striped one.

That is how Chipmunk got his stripes. Ever since then, Chipmunk has been the first animal to get up every morning. As the sun rises, he scoots to the top of the tallest tree to sing his song:

"The sun came up,
the sun came up,
the sun came up,
the sun came up!"

And ever since then, Bear has been the last animal to get up. He doesn't like to hear Chipmunk's song. It reminds him—as it reminds us all—that no one, not even Bear, can do everything.